THE LITTLE
TOY ENGINE
AND OTHER STORIES

The Little Toy Engine

and Other Stories

by
ENID BLYTON

Illustrated by
Dorothy Hamilton

AWARD PUBLICATIONS

For further information on Enid Blyton please contact www.blyton.co

ISBN 0-86163-410-1

Text copyright 1951 The Enid Blyton Company
Illustrations copyright © 1989 Award Publications Limited

Enid Blyton's signature is a trademark of The Enid Blyton Company

This edition entitled *The Little Toy Engine and Other Stories*
published by permission of The Enid Blyton Company

First published 1989
12th impression 2001

Published by Award Publications Limited,
27 Longford Street,London NW1 3DZ

Printed in Singapore

CONTENTS

Corovell, the Children's Dustman

Once upon a time, long, long ago, the world became so full of exciting happenings that the children could not go to sleep at night. Mothers and fathers began to get worried. The fairies too were anxious, for when a child did not sleep, he became cross and tired, and, of course, could not see any fairies. And the fairies did not like that at all, for they loved playing with the children.

So the King of the Fairies called a great meeting, to which all the fairies, big and little, came.

'I will offer a reward,' said the king, 'to any fairy who can find something to make all the children go to sleep at the proper time.'

All the fairies were very excited and they

began to make plans at once.

'I know what I shall do,' said one. 'I shall string some baby stars together, and hold them in front of the children's eyes. They will be so dazzled with starshine that they will fall asleep at once!'

'I don't think much of that idea,' said another fairy. 'I'm going to hunt up the magic words in an old book and make them into a sleep-song. Then I shall sing it, and all the children will go to sleep, listening.'

Each fairy had a different idea, and each began to try to do what he had planned. The necklace of baby stars was no use, for the brightness made the children more awake than ever. The

magic sleep-song *did* send some of them to sleep, but it kept others awake.

Another fairy tried stroking the children's hair very softly; but while it brought sleep to some, it fidgeted others. Others danced softly round the candle in the children's bedroom, but they were so interested in watching the fairies that they were wider awake than ever.

The fairies began to feel there was really *nothing* to be done, and one by one they gave up trying. Great gloom settled over Fairyland, for the tired children were much too cross ever to play with the fairies in the daytime.

Now all this time there was one little fairy, called Corovell, who was very

busy indeed. All one day he was scraping the bloom off the darkest red roses he could find in Fairyland, and shaking it down into a yellow sack he was carrying. On another day he went to all the blue butterflies he knew, and begged them each to give him a little powder from one of their wings. Because they liked little Corovell, they shook some of their powder into his outstretched hands, and flew off into the sunshine. Corovell carefully mixed it with the rose bloom in his sack.

The next morning he scraped the sunshine from the top of all the little puddles shining in the sun. This he mixed carefully with some black powder from the middle of bright red poppies.

He took the softest and brightest green moss growing on the palace wall, and powdered it into tiny, tiny pieces. Then he mixed into it the magic scent of the June wild roses, and shook it all up together with the other powders and dust. As he was carrying the sack along

through the wood that night he picked
out a star shining in a puddle and put it
into his sack, just for luck. To finish off,
he stirred it all up well with the brightest green feather from a kingfisher's
breast.

When Corovell was satisfied with his
mixture, he took his yellow sack on his
shoulders and went to the king's
palace.

'Your Majesty,' he said, bowing low,
'I have discovered something which
will make any child sleepy.'

'Prove it,' said the king eagerly.

Corovell flew to a nursery full of naughty, tired children.

'Now watch,' he said softly. He dipped his hand into his sack, and pulling out a handful of glittering dust, he flung some of it into each child's eyes.

The baby child fell asleep at once. The next smallest crept over to her mother, and laying her head down, went to sleep. All the other children stopped quarrelling and began to rub their eyes, saying, 'Oh, I *am* so sleepy.'

'Well done!' said the king. 'It is a wonderful discovery. What is your sleep-dust made of?'

Corovell told him. 'And,' he said, 'it not only makes the children go to sleep, but it makes them dream of roses and butterflies and poppies and starshine – all the beautiful things in the world.'

'Splendid!' cried the king. 'The children will soon be happy in the daytime now, so that we can play with them again. What will you have for your reward?'

'Make me the children's Dust-man,' asked the little fairy, kneeling down before the king. 'Grant that I may be their special night-time friend, and that they may all know and love me.'

'Very well, that shall be your reward,' answered the king. 'You shall be the children's Dust-man, and make the children sleepy at night-time, so that the next day they will not be too tired to see us when we come to play with them.'

And every night since then, as quick as the gleam on a dragonfly's wing, along comes the Dust-man with his yellow sack of magic sleep-dust. He flings some of it into every child's eyes, and they grow sleepier and sleepier, and at last fall softly asleep, to dream of flowers and birds, butterflies and star-shine, until daytime peeps in through the window.

The Little Toy Engine

'Where are you, twins?' called Mother. 'Johnny, Jenny! Where are you?'

'Here, Mummy!' shouted the twins. 'Oh, are you going out? Take us too.'

'Not this morning,' said Mother. 'I'm in a hurry.'

'Well, we'll be in a hurry too,' said Jenny. 'We'll rush along like anything.'

'No, dear,' said Mother. 'I want you to stay at home–but for a real treat Granny has said that you can go and help her make cakes.'

'*Has she!*' said Johnny, very pleased. 'Oooh–we can scrape out the bowl and have a currant or two. . .'

'And eat a bit of candied peel, and do some stirring, and measure out the sugar and flour,' said Jenny. 'I don't mind not coming out with you, Mummy, if I can be with Granny when she's making cakes.'

Mother went off, smiling. The twins rushed into the kitchen. 'Granny! Mummy says you'll let us help you make cakes this morning.'

Granny beamed at them. She was so nice and round and plump, and her face was always so pink and her eyes so blue and twinkly.

'I shall work you hard!' she said. 'You'll have to measure out the things for me, and taste the currants and sultanas to see if they're all right, and I'm going to make a jelly too. Can either of you put the wobble into a jelly for me?'

'Goodness, do you have to mix wobble into jellies?' said Jenny, in surprise, 'I never knew that before!'

Granny chuckled. 'There's lots of things you don't know yet,' she said. 'Now look, do you see what I've got for helpful children? Look over there!'

The children looked over to the dresser. On it stood two tiny toys. One was the tiniest, prettiest little toy engine, no bigger than Jenny's little finger, and the other was a little toy dog.

'Have you *really* got those for us?' said Johnny, picking up the toy engine. 'I think I'll have this engine, it's marvellous!'

'I might like that,' said Jenny at once. 'I might choose that.'

'Engines are for boys, not girls,' said Johnny. 'It would be a waste of an engine for you to have this. You can have the little dog.'

'Now, now,' said Granny, beginning to bustle round. 'You've neither of you done

a thing yet, to earn your rewards, so it's no good choosing, you mightn't have either!'

Well, you should have seen how busy those twins were that morning! Granny said she wanted fifty raisins, fifty sultanas and one hundred currants counted out properly, and mixed together for the big cake. She said she wanted the candied peel cut into tiny bits. She said she wanted the mixture stirred and stirred.

So Johnny began counting, and Jenny began too. Jenny finished first, because she really was *very* good at counting. Poor Johnny got halfway through his counting, and then he spilt most of the packet on the floor!

'Oh dear! It will take ages to pick up all these!' he said.

'You'll have to wash them, too,' said Granny. 'We can't use things straight off the floor.'

Jenny took the candied peel and cut it into tiny little bits. 'You can pop a bit into your mouth each time you have cut twelve bits,' said Granny. That was very nice indeed!

'I've finished all the peel for you,' said Jenny. 'Now I'll help you stir.'

'You've done so well that I really think you can have your reward now,' said Granny.

'Johnny's doing quite well, but he hasn't finished his jobs yet. So you can choose first, Jenny.'

'Then I'll have the tiny toy engine, please,' said Jenny, and she took it off the dresser. Johnny looked as black as thunder.

'I wanted that,' he said. 'You know I did. I shall take it away from you! An engine is a boy's toy, not a girl's.'

'It's mine,' said Jenny, 'and you're not

to take it away. Is he, Granny?'

'Of course not,' said Granny. But she knew that Johnny *might* try to snatch it, so she put Jenny the other side of the table. She stood the little toy engine on the top of a tin of baking powder.

'There! It can watch you doing some more jobs for me!' she said. 'Will you take the stones out of the dates?'

Johnny went on with his jobs, sulking. Jenny took the stones out of the dates. It was a sticky job but a nice one because her fingers tasted lovely when she licked them. The little toy engine stood on the tin, looking really sweet. Jenny felt very pleased with it indeed.

'I've done my share of the dates,' she said to Granny. 'Now, what's next? This is a really lovely morning of work, Granny. I *am* enjoying myself.'

'Will you empty some brown sugar out of the bag into that sugar basin?' said Granny. 'You have it on your porridge in the morning, and the basin is almost empty.'

'I want to do that,' said Johnny. But

Jenny snatched up the bag of brown sugar and began shaking the big brown grains into the breakfast basin.

Johnny bumped hard against the table, to make Jenny spill the sugar, and quite a lot went on the top of the table.

'Don't!' said Jenny. 'Now I've spilt it!'

She scraped up the sugar, and then emptied the rest of it into the basin. It filled it nicely to the top.

'It makes me feel hungry for porridge

this very minute!' said Jenny. 'Oh look– there's Mummy coming home again!'

She ran to the window and waved. 'Come round to the kitchen door, Mummy!' she called. 'We're here!'

Mother came in smiling. 'Well, have you been busy?' she said. 'What have you done?'

Johnny and Jenny told her. 'And oh, Mummy,' said Jenny, 'do, do look at the dear little toy engine Granny has given me.'

She went to the table to get it but it wasn't there. Jenny looked all over the table. Then she looked at Johnny.

'You've taken my engine!' she said. 'You horrid naughty boy! You've taken it!'

'I haven't,' said Johnny, going very red in the face, and looking very angry indeed.

'You have, you have!' said Jenny. 'Mummy, you ought to scold Johnny. He's taken my engine!'

'Now, now, now!' said Mother. 'This is all very silly. Come into the other room with me, and we'll find out what has happened to it!'

So into the sitting-room they went, Jenny almost in tears, and Johnny looking very, very cross.

'Now,' said Mother, 'WHAT has happened to the little toy engine?'

It really wasn't much good Mother asking about the little engine. Jenny said Johnny had taken it, and Johnny stamped his foot and said he hadn't.

'Then it simply must still be in the

24

kitchen,' said Mother. 'We'll go back and look.'

So back they went. Granny had cleared up all the things on the kitchen table by then, and she shook her head when Mother came in.

'There's no little engine,' she said. 'I looked everywhere on the table and on the floor too. But it's certainly gone.'

'Johnny's taken it, I know he has,' said Jenny. 'He *keeps* saying he hasn't, but I'm sure he's got it in his pocket.'

'I haven't,' said Johnny. 'And I don't ever tell stories, do I, Mummy?'

'No, you don't,' said Mother. Granny agreed. 'He doesn't,' she said. 'They're both truthful children. Jenny, you'll have to believe Johnny. I'm sure he means what he says. Johnny, you must have your reward for your good work too, take the little toy dog, dear.'

Johnny took it, beaming suddenly. He had thought he wasn't going to have anything because the engine had disappeared. Jenny began to cry.

'It isn't fair!' she sobbed. 'I did better

work than Johnny, and I was quicker too, and now my engine's gone, and Johnny's got the dog. It isn't fair.'

Johnny hated to see Jenny cry. He stood and stared at her. 'Jenny,' he said, suddenly, 'please say that you believe I didn't take your engine. Please say it.'

Jenny wiped her eyes and looked at her twin. 'All right,' she said, at last. 'I don't believe you took my engine. But I do think it's very, very peculiar, the way it disappeared.'

'Oh, I'm *glad* you believe me!' cried Johnny, and he ran over to Jenny. 'Have my dog to make up for your lost engine. Take it–it's a dear little thing.'

'Oh!' said Jenny, in surprise. 'You *are* nice, Johnny. But you'd better keep the dog yourself.'

'No, you have him,' said Johnny. 'You can give him back to me if Granny finds the engine anywhere. Don't cry any more, Jenny.'

So Jenny dried her eyes and took the little dog. Mother looked at Granny and Granny smiled back. 'He's a good little fellow, our Johnny,' she said, and Mother nodded.

Well, when Mother swept up the kitchen, she looked EVERYWHERE for the little toy engine, because she was just as puzzled as everyone else. But it wasn't found. So Jenny put the little dog on her mantelpiece, and Johnny tried not to wish he had had a reward to keep, too.

And next morning a most surprising thing happened. Mother and Father and the twins all sat down to breakfast as usual. Mother lifted up the lid of the porridge pot and ladled out porridge for everyone. Then she poured out coffee for herself and Father, and milk for the twins.

'Pass the brown sugar, please, Jenny,' said her father. 'Help yourself first.'

'No, *you* first, Daddy,' said Jenny, and she pushed the basin across. Her father dipped in the spoon and took a large helping. He was very fond of brown sugar.

He scattered it over his porridge and put the spoon back. Then he looked down at his porridge, frowning in surprise.

'What a remarkable thing!' he said. 'Now where in the world did *that* come from?'

'What?' asked the twins. Father dipped his spoon into his porridge, and

held it out to the twins.

'This!' he said. 'A tiny little toy engine sitting on the top of my porridge, with brown sugar all round it! What an extraordinary thing!'

The twins gave such a loud yell that their mother jumped in fright.

'My toy engine!' shouted Jenny. 'Look, look, it's come back again!'

'But how?' cried Johnny, in excitement. 'It must be magic!'

'Well, well, well!' said Mother. 'What a very surprising thing. HOW did it come to be on Daddy's porridge?'

'I know! I know!' shouted Johnny.

'Jenny, do you remember you were pouring brown sugar into the basin yesterday when I bumped the table hard? Well, the little engine must have jumped straight off the top of the tin when I bumped, and it fell into the sugar basin and you never noticed! *That's* where it disappeared to!'

'Of course!' said Jenny, staring at the little engine. 'That's exactly what must have happened. And I said you'd taken

it. Oh dear, I'm very sorry, Johnny.'

'But you believed me when I said I didn't take it,' said Johnny, 'didn't you? Now you know I *really* didn't. I can have the little dog back, can't I?'

Jenny stared at him. 'No,' she said suddenly. 'You can't have the dog back. You're going to have the engine, Johnny! You wanted it, but I took it, and then I was horrid to you. You're to have the engine!'

'I think he should,' said Mother. 'He gave up the dog because he didn't like to see you crying, Jenny, and I think he

31

deserves this little engine.'

Jenny took it off Father's spoon, wiped it carefully and stood it by Johnny's plate. 'There you are,' she said. 'And I'm *glad* you're having it, I think you're a very nice twin.'

They ran to tell Granny after breakfast.

'Well!' she said, 'that really was a surprising thing – but it's all ended well, with everybody happy. And that's how it should be.'

The tiny engine sits on the mantelpiece with the little dog beside him.

The Crown of Gold

Once upon a time there was a fairy who was very sad. He sat in a yellow celandine, and swayed to and fro, thinking about everything. Two big tears rolled down his cheeks, and trickled down the stalk of the celandine.

'Oh dear, oh dear!' he sighed.

'What ever is the matter?' said a brimstone butterfly, out for the first time that spring.

'Oh,' answered Casilda, the little fairy, 'I'm sad because I don't do anything so well as the other fairies can. I can't make beautiful dresses from morning mist like Sylfai, I can't paint the sunset pink, and I can't even hang the dewdrops on the grasses without spilling them.'

'That is very sad,' said the butterfly. 'But what does it matter?'

'Well, you see,' explained Casilda, 'every summer our king holds his court, and gives little silver crowns set with pearls to all those fairies who do beautiful work. *All* my friends have got crowns, but I never win one, however hard I try.'

'Cheer up,' said the butterfly, 'there are other things worth while doing, even if you don't win a crown for them!'

'Oh, *what*?' exclaimed Casilda.

'Why, go into the world of boys and girls and see if you can't help the people there a bit,' said the butterfly. 'There's always lots of things to be done, even if you can't do them really well.'

'I'll go at once!' cried Casilda, standing up in the swaying celandine. 'Good-bye, yellow butterfly, and thank you!' Off he flew, out of Fairyland and into our world.

The first thing he came to there was a clothes-line pegged with clothes. Mr Wind was tugging at one beautiful

frock, and trying his hardest to pull it down into the mud.

'You *are* in a bad mood today, Mr Wind!' cried Casilda. He flew on to the clothes-line, and sat down by the frock, holding it tight. Mr Wind tugged and tugged, and very nearly made the little fairy tumble off. Then out of the house hobbled an old woman.

When she saw Casilda she cried out with pleasure. 'Oh, thank you,' she said, 'if you hadn't held the frock on the line for me, little fairy, the wind would have whisked it away, and I should have had to wash it clean again. My poor old back is tired of stooping to wash, so thank you very much.'

'Don't mention it,' called Casilda, flying off again.

The next day Casilda heard a tiny child crying bitterly because his balloon had blown away, and he could not reach it.

'Never mind,' said Casilda. 'Watch me get it!' and off he flew up into the air, caught the string, and flew down

again. The balloon came down with the string, and the child was delighted.

'Oh, thank you, dear little fairy,' he said gratefully.

'Don't mention it,' said Casilda, flying away.

Another time Casilda, peeping in at a window of a little house, saw a woman crying. She was holding her head, and saying, 'Oh, my head *does* hurt so.'

'What ever can I do for her?' thought Casilda. 'I can't think of anything.' He looked round the room and noticed how dirty and dark it was.

I know, he thought; the room wants brightening up. I'll get some flowers.

Off he flew to the meadows, and brought back a lovely bunch of golden buttercups and white daisies. He

dropped them into the woman's lap. She was so astonished that she stopped crying, and forgot all about her bad headache.

'How lovely!' she cried, 'and how dark and dirty the room looks now with these bright flowers in it. I must hurry up and clean it.'

So she put the flowers in water, and started cleaning the room, singing cheerfully.

Casilda flew away feeling very pleased with himself. 'Tomorrow is the day our king holds his court and gives those lovely crowns,' he said to himself. 'I shall have to go, but I shan't mind a bit not winning a crown, because I've found something else I can do to make myself happy.'

Every fairy came to the king's palace the next day. The king was on his throne, and by him were many little silver crowns set with pearls. There was also one little golden crown set with diamonds, and Casilda wondered whether any of his friends had won it.

'Do you think you've won a crown this year?' asked Sylfai, the fairy dress-maker.

'Oh no,' answered Casilda, 'I know I haven't, because I've stopped doing beautiful things, and I live in the world of boys and girls now.'

Then the king made a speech, and said how glad he was to have the crowns to give to fairies who had done beautiful things that year.

'Peronel,' he called. 'Here is a crown for you. You did a most beautiful thing when you painted the almond blossom such a lovely pink this spring.'

Peronel proudly received the crown.

'Morfael,' said the king. 'This crown is given to you for ringing the bluebells so sweetly at our last dance.'

Morfael went up for his crown most delighted. Then one by one the king gave out all his crowns except the gold one.

'This crown,' he said, 'is for a little fairy who gave up doing beautiful things in Fairyland, but went all by himself into the world of boys and girls and did beautiful things there. He didn't think they were beautiful, but they were, and we are very proud of him. Casilda, here is your crown.'

You can just imagine how pleased Casilda was, and what a lovely surprise

The Crown of Gold

he had. He is the only fairy in Fairyland who wears a golden crown, so if you meet a fairy wearing one, you will know at once that it is Casilda.

When The Bus Was Full

Johnny and Jenny had been to Granny's for tea. They had had a lovely time. Granny had a new kitten and they had played with it, and she had let them play with Grandpa's old soldiers for a treat as well.

The soldiers were big and heavy, and not a bit like the ones Johnny had at home. He liked them very much. So did the kitten. It kept running at them and knocking them down.

Granny's house was fun. She had a cuckoo-clock with a wooden cuckoo that popped out of its little house to flap its wings and cry 'Cuckoo' every half-hour – and she had a little Chinaman who nodded his head for hours when he was tapped.

'I never like saying goodbye when I come to tea with you, Granny,' said Jenny, when Granny said it was time for the twins to catch the bus. 'I really like everything here.'

'Well, you wouldn't like not to go home,' said Granny, smiling. 'Now, you really must go. If you miss the bus you would have such a very long way to walk home – and soon it will be dark.'

The twins kissed Granny goodbye and set off to the bus-stop. There were quite a lot of people waiting for the bus, and the twins took their place at the end of the queue. They were the last, except for a bent old woman, when the bus at last came rumbling round the corner.

'I hope there'll be room for us!' said Jenny, as everyone got in one by one. 'It looks very full!'

'Two more!' called the conductor. 'Two more only. Get in, little girl. Jump up, young man. Sorry, madam – I'm afraid you'll have to wait for the next bus!'

Jenny got in safely – and Johnny was just climbing in, too, when he heard what the conductor said. The last person of all, the bent old lady, was to be left behind! There was no room for her.

He scrambled off at once. 'Wait, wait!' he called to the conductor, 'I'll walk. Help this old lady on. Don't go without her!'

'Oh, Johnny! It's such a long way home – and it's getting dark. You'll get lost!' shouted Jenny, trying to get out of the bus too. But the conductor pushed her back.

'Now, now – the bus is just going. No

getting off after I've rung the bell!'

With a jerk the bus started, and left Johnny standing alone on the pavement. Jenny's eyes filled with tears. Johnny would have such a long way to walk home. It would be dark – their mother would

be worried – and Johnny would be very late back. Oh dear!

'You've a kind brother,' said the old lady. 'Very kind. It isn't many children who bother about old ladies now. I'm sorry he had to be left behind. Look – you give him this when you get home, with my love!'

She pushed a little tin of toffees into Jenny's hand. 'Go on now, take it – that brother of yours deserves a little treat.'

'Thank you. I'll give him the tin,' said Jenny, thinking that Johnny would be very pleased, because his favourite toffees were inside.

The bus rumbled along fast, and in twenty minutes Jenny was home. She sped indoors, calling to her mother.

'Mummy! Johnny didn't get the bus! He gave up his place to an old lady. Mummy, he'll be very late and it's dark already. Shall we go to meet him?'

'But Johnny's home!' said Mother's voice, from upstairs.

'No, he's not!' shouted Jenny. 'I left him at the bus-stop. He's walking back in the dark.'

'But darling – I heard Johnny whistling quite a long time ago!' said Mother. 'And look – there is his cap –and his coat too!'

Jenny stared at the cap and coat in

surprise. 'But - but - I left Johnny at the bus-stop!' she said. 'I did really. Johnny CAN'T be home!'

'Well, call him and see,' said her mother. So Jenny called loudly:

'Johnny! JOHNNY! You're not at home, are you?'

A loud shout came down from Johnny's bedroom. 'HELLO! That you, Jenny? Yes, I'm home all right. I raced you, didn't I?'

Jenny was too surprised to speak. She ran to the stairs and there was Johnny waiting at the top.

'But - but - how did you race the bus?' she said. 'It went quite fast. Johnny, tell me, did you run all the way or something?'

Johnny grinned. 'I'll tell you what happened,' he said. 'A man coming out of a nearby house saw me give up my seat to that old lady - and he came up and said, "Like a lift, young man?" And I saw that it was our doctor, Dr Browne!'

'Oh, what luck!' said Jenny.

'Yes. And I said: "Please, if you're

going my way, and it's no trouble to you, sir," and he said: "One good turn deserves another. This is my good turn. Hop in!" So I hopped in, and he whizzed me home!'

'Did you pass the bus?' asked Jenny.

'Rather! I saw you in the corner seat and thought what a surprise you'd have!' said Johnny, with a grin. 'What's that you've got in your hand?'

'A tin of your favourite toffees,' said Jenny. 'From that old woman. She said you deserved a present.'

'How kind of her!' said Johnny. 'But I don't deserve a present, because I got a lift home! Let's open the tin and share the toffees. And let's go and offer one to

Mummy.'

Their mother listened to the little tale of the full-up bus as she took a toffee and unwrapped it.

'Nice boy!' she said to Johnny. 'You're always kind to your own granny – and I'm glad to know you're kind to someone else's granny too. You deserve the toffees!'

He did, didn't he, and I'm very glad he had them!

The Boy Who Didn't Believe

There was once a little boy called Jim who didn't believe in fairies. The fairies didn't mind at all, and really never thought about him. But the gnomes, who sometimes hid themselves in his garden, grew very angry when they heard him one day singing a song he had made up himself—

> 'There aren't any gnomes or fairies,
>   Or witches or giants tall;
> There are not any goblins or pixies,
>   There's nothing like that at all!'

That was what Jim sang as he wandered round his garden.

'Stupid little boy!' snorted the gnomes who were listening. 'Let's punish him for making up such a horrid song!'

THIS WAY TO
THE
WISHING WELL

'Yes, let's,' said the leader. 'And I know how – let's put him into Fairyland, and tell him to find his way home! He'll keep meeting people he doesn't believe in, and he *will* get such a shock!'

All the gnomes thought it would be a splendid idea, and when Jim came near them they threw themselves on him, blindfolded his eyes, and led him straight into Fairyland.

'Oh, oh! Let me go, let me go!' cried Jim, very frightened.

'*We'll* let you go!' chuckled the gnomes, as they took away the handkerchief from his eyes.

'Where am I?' asked Jim, looking around; but the gnomes had vanished, and he was quite alone.

'What a funny thing!' said Jim to himself. 'Whoever did that to me? And wherever am I?'

He was standing in the middle of a field which was full of the loveliest flowers he had ever seen. By him was a signpost on which was painted—

THIS WAY TO THE WISHING WELL

'Well, I may as well go along to the wishing well,' decided Jim, 'and perhaps I shall find out the way home.'

He followed a little winding path across the field until he came to a stile. To his surprise there was a large yel-

low bird on the top. It perched there and looked at him, without attempting to fly away.

'You lovely tame thing!' said Jim, stroking its shiny feathers. 'But how am I to get over the stile, I wonder, with you sitting on top?'

'Why didn't you say you wanted to get over?' asked the bird, flying into the hedge nearby.

Jim nearly jumped out of his skin! He looked at the bird as if he couldn't believe his eyes.

'What are you staring at me like that for?' asked the yellow bird, in an angry voice.

'My goodness!' exclaimed Jim, finding his tongue again. 'Well!! Goodness gracious!!! Whoever heard of a bird talking like that before?'

'Don't be silly,' said the yellow bird, 'you know you're in Fairyland, where all the birds can talk!'

'In Fairyland!' cried Jim. 'But I can't be; there isn't such a place!'

'You *are* a silly boy!' remarked the bird crossly. 'Fancy saying there isn't such a place when you're there all the time!'

'Well, I *don't* believe in Fairyland. Would you please tell me the way home?'

But the yellow bird only snorted at

him in disgust, and flew away over the field.

This *is* a funny place, and no mistake! thought Jim, climbing over the stile into the next field.

In the middle of the field was a funny, higgledy-piggledy well, and sitting on the wall round it was a pretty little fairy dressed in mauve.

Jim rubbed his eyes and pinched himself.

'It *can't* be a fairy!' he said. 'It simply can't! It must be somebody dressed up like one.'

He ran up to the well. 'What are you dressed up like a fairy for?' he asked the little mauve fairy.

She looked puzzled. 'I *am* a fairy,' she answered.

'But there aren't any fairies!' said Jim. 'So you can't be one.'

'You're a silly little boy,' said the fairy, rather crossly. 'You're in Fairyland, where there are *lots* of fairies!'

'Well, I *don't* believe in fairies,' said Jim, 'and I'll sing you the little song I made up about them.'

Jim began singing—

'There aren't any gnomes or fairies—'

'Hush! hush!' cried the mauve fairy, 'you mustn't sing things like that here! You'll have the Lord High Chamberlain of Fairyland after you, and he'll turn you into a frog or something.'

Jim stopped and looked rather frightened. Then he saw someone clambering over the stile in the distance, waving a stick and shouting.

'Oh dear! Is that the Lord High Chamberlain?' he asked.

'Yes, it is! Oh, goodness me, how can I save you! He looks terribly angry!' cried the mauve fairy.

Jim was so frightened that, without thinking what he was doing, he jumped straight into the wishing well! He fell down and down and down, until at last, *splash*! He was in water up to his waist.

'Where's that boy gone?' he heard the chamberlain roaring. '*I'll* teach him to sing songs like that in Fairyland! I'll teach him!'

After a little while Jim saw the mauve fairy leaning over the top of the well.

'He's gone!' she called; 'but he and the yellow bird are looking for you all over the place.'

'Whatever shall I do?' asked poor Jim.

'Well, there's only one thing left for you to do; you must go and ask the queen to forgive you and let you go home,' said the mauve fairy.

'How can I get to her?' asked Jim.

'Let me think. You can't come up here again, for the yellow bird will see you. You must go through the underground passages till you come to the rushing lift,' advised the fairy. 'Anyone will tell you the way from there. You'll find a little door let into the well wall if you climb up a few steps.'

Jim found the steps, climbed up a little way, and discovered a door.

'I've found it,' he called. 'Thank you very much for helping me.'

'Goodbye!' cried the fairy, waving to him.

Jim opened the door, and found himself in a narrow passage, lighted by one large lantern hung on a nail. He took it down to carry with him.

He went for a good way and eventually he came to a door.

'It sounds as if there's someone crying inside there!' said Jim, listening.

He pushed open the door and looked in. Sitting on a stool was a little gnome, sobbing as if his heart would break.

'What's the matter?' asked Jim in a kind voice.

'Oh dear!' sobbed the gnome. 'My lamp has gone out and I can't finish my work, and it *must* be done this evening.'

'Well, have my lantern,' said Jim, feeling sorry for the little gnome.

'Oh, can you spare it? Thank you so much!' cried the gnome happily. 'Now I can finish my work!'

Jim went out of the room, into the dark passage again, and this time he had to *feel* his way about, for he had no lantern. He was rather frightened, but he tried to pretend he wasn't.

At last he came into a well-lighted passage, where a lot of animals hurried to and fro. There were rabbits, hedgehogs, moles, and hares, and they all looked very busy.

'Where are you going?' Jim asked a grey rabbit, who was dragging a very large sack.

'To market!' panted the rabbit. 'It's market day in Oak Tree Town today. Oh dear! This sack *is* so heavy.'

'I'll help you,' said Jim, and put the heavy sack on his shoulder, whilst the rabbit ran beside him.

Presently they came to a big purple chair.

'This is the rushing lift,' explained the rabbit, sitting down on the chair.

'Good! I want to go up in it!' exclaimed Jim, and sat down beside the rabbit.

Whiz-z-z-z! Whoosh!! Up went the chair at such a tremendous pace that Jim could hardly breathe.

At the top was a large garden and nearby a great palace.

'That's the queen's palace,' said the grey rabbit, 'and oh, my goodness! Here's the queen herself in the garden!'

Jim saw a tall and beautiful lady with great blue wings standing near him. He went up to her and knelt down on one knee.

'Please, your Majesty,' he said, 'I'm the boy who sang that horrid song, and will you forgive me, because I'm sorry?'

Suddenly the Lord High Chamberlain rushed up, and the yellow bird flew down.

'No, *don't* forgive him, your Majesty. He doesn't believe in fairies! He's a horrid boy!' they cried.

'He's a *kind* boy,' cried the grey rabbit, 'he carried my heavy sack.'

'Yes,' said another voice, 'and he lent me his lantern to see by when my lamp went out.' It was the little gnome Jim had heard crying. He had suddenly appeared from somewhere with Jim's lantern.

The Boy Who Didn't Believe

'Do you believe in fairies?' asked the queen gently.

'Oh *yes*, I do now!' cried Jim; 'and I'm sorry I've been so silly and horrid. *Please* don't let the chamberlain punish me!'

'Well, he was going to,' said the queen, 'but as I hear you've been so kind to two of my people, I'm going to forgive you.'

'Oh, thank you!' cried Jim. 'And may I go home soon?'

The queen waved her wand.

Everything grew mistier and mistier. The queen faded, and the chamberlain—

Then suddenly everything grew bright again!

'Hurray!' cried Jim. 'I'm in my own garden! And *what* an adventure I've had! I'll *never* say I don't believe in fairies again!'

And you should have heard the gnomes nearby chuckling when they heard that!

Morning Mist and Starshine

'I want that dress most particularly for Wednesday night,' said the Fairy Queen to Sylfai, the fairy dressmaker.

'Yes, Your Majesty,' answered Sylfai, sewing busily.

'What should you like in return for making me such a lovely dress?' asked the queen kindly. 'You can have anything you like.'

'Oh, Your Majesty, *do* you think I might come to the dance on Wednesday night?' begged Sylfai. 'I should so love to see you wearing this lovely dress; it's the prettiest one I've ever made.'

'Yes, you shall come,' answered the queen. 'I'll send you an invitation; but mind, you must have on your very best dress, and you must look your very loveliest, because my cousin, the Prince of Dreamland, is coming, and I want everyone to look their best.'

'Of course,' promised Sylfai. 'I'll put on all my best things, and shine up my wings beautifully.'

The Fairy Queen then departed, and left Sylfai happily at work. She was making a truly wonderful dress. Her thread was finest spider's web, and her stitches so small, it was quite impossible to see them. The dress was made of blue morning mist and embroidered with starshine, with a little rosette of baby forget-me-not blooms at the waist. No one but Sylfai could have made it, for only she knew how to make up morning mist and starshine into dresses.

All that day she sewed, and all the next. The rabbits came and watched her. They thought she was very clever.

'Can we do anything to help you, Sylfai?' they asked. 'Can we fetch you more spider's web?'

'Yes, please,' answered Sylfai, 'only

be sure the spider has finished with it first. And when you come back, perhaps the squirrel will wind it on my reel for me.'

'Oh yes,' said the squirrel, who loved busy little Sylfai.

But the rabbits came back saying the

spiders would not give them any more silken thread.

'Nonsense!' said Sylfai, jumping up. 'You can't have told them it was for the queen's dress. I'll go and see for myself; please look after the dress for me,' and off she flew.

The rabbits and the squirrel sat round to guard the dress, but alas, the wind came by, shook the dress of morning mist as it lay on the grass, and then whisked it up into the air, and away over the tops of the trees!

'Oh dear! Oh dear!' said the rabbits.

'Oh dear! Oh dear!' sighed the squirrel.

'Oh dear! Oh dear!' sobbed Sylfai, when she came back and heard the sad news.

'Never mind,' said the squirrel hopefully. 'Tell the queen you couldn't help it, and put on your best dress and go to the dance just the same!'

'Oh no, I couldn't,' wept Sylfai. 'I *promised* the queen she should have her dress tonight, and I'd made it so beautifully too! I shall go after the wind and see if I can get back the dress!'

Off she went, up into the air, searching all round for the frock of morning mist, but nowhere could she see it. She flew for miles and miles, and at last came to the home of the South Wind.

'Please,' she said, 'tell me where you put the dress you whisked away this morning.'

'Dear me, was it an important one?' said the South Wind.

'Yes, very. Oh, *do* tell me what you

71

did with it,' cried Sylfai impatiently.

'Well, to tell you the truth, I don't know,' said the South Wind. 'I'm very sorry, but I never thought about it.'

'Oh dear! oh dear!' said Sylfai sadly. 'You really *should* look what you're doing, you know.'

Off she flew again on the way home. She was very tired, and soon, to give her wings a rest, she began to walk through the wood. As she went along she heard a little frightened voice say:

'Please, could you take me home?'

Sylfai saw a tiny little fairy, whose wings were not even properly grown.

'Well, I'm in a great hurry,' she said, 'but tell me where your home is, and I'll take you there.'

'Oh, thank you,' said the tiny fairy, gratefully.

When they arrived at the birch tree where he lived, the tiny fairy's mother came out to thank Sylfai.

'Would you like to see what I found in the wood today?' she asked Sylfai. 'The South Wind brought it, and it's beautiful.' She opened a cupboard and took out something blue and shimmering.

'Oh,' gasped Sylfai, in delight, 'it's the Fairy Queen's dress! Give it to me quickly; I may be able to get it to her in time!'

Sylfai flew along as fast as she could, hot and panting, feeling her dress torn by brambles and her hair pulled by thorns. At last, tired, dirty, and torn, she arrived at the palace, and asked to see the queen. She was taken into the magnificent great hall, where

everyone was assembled.

'Oh dear!' said Sylfai. 'I didn't know the party had begun! I've brought the queen's dress for her, and now it's too late!'

'Sylfai,' said the queen, in great surprise, 'what do you mean by coming to my party dressed like that, and so untidy too!'

Sylfai burst into tears. Kneeling down before the queen she told all the story of the lost dress and how it was found. 'And I *didn't* mean to come to the party,' she said; 'I've only brought the dress.'

'Poor little Sylfai!' said the queen. 'You *shall* come to the party. Go and wash your face, and put on the very dress you made for *me*! Such a kind little fairy deserves the most beautiful dress in the world.'

You can just imagine how pleased Sylfai was, and everyone said that, after the queen, Sylfai looked the sweetest little fairy there, in her beautiful dress of morning mist and starshine.

My Nut I Think!

The squirrel was collecting nuts for his winter hoard. He had a nice little hiding-place in a hole in his tree.

But the nuthatch found the hoard.

The nuthatch was a fine looking bird with a very strong beak and he was just as fond of nuts as the squirrel was.

He didn't sit up and gnaw a hole in the shell to get at the kernel, as the squirrel did. No, he hadn't teeth like the squirrel. He tackled the nut in a different way.

He took it in his beak and wedged it tightly in a ridge in the bark of a tree.

Then, clinging fast to the trunk, he hammered hard at the shell with his strong, powerful beak.

Crack! He broke the shell and then

ate the nut inside. Delicious!

Now the squirrel was asleep one day, when the nuthatch began to hammer at a nut in the very same tree as the sleeping squirrel. The squirrel woke up with a jump and put his head out of the hole to see what the noise was.

He saw the nut in the bark of the tree

and felt annoyed. He ran down to it and began to try and get it out with his little paw.

'My nut, I think!' he said.

'No, *my* nut!' said the nuthatch and gave the nut a peck. It fell to the ground.

The squirrel flew at the nuthatch, who at once tried to peck him.

Now, after that, to annoy the squirrel, the nuthatch always hammered at nuts just below his sleeping-hole and woke him up.

To make matters worse, he always

chose nuts out of the squirrel's own hoard.

So, time after time, the squirrel would wake up, leap from his hole and cry, 'My nut, I think!' And then there would be a squabble and the nut would fall to the ground.

'I can find the nuts afterwards,' thought the squirrel.

'I will pick up the nuts another time,' thought the nuthatch. 'What fun it is to annoy this sleepy little squirrel!'

Now, at the bottom of the tree, in a small hole, lived a little mouse. Like the

My Nut I Think!

squirrel he hoarded food for the cold days, but he hadn't very much that winter. So when he found nuts falling round him day after day, he was very surprised and pleased.

'There's a lot of hammering and jabbering going on up there!' he thought, looking up into the tree.

'Somebody seems to be throwing away nuts all the time!'

When the squirrel went down to collect his nuts, they weren't there! Not one was to be found. The nuthatch flew down too and began to look.

'We'll share them,' he said to the squirrel. 'I won't tease you any more.'

But there were no nuts to be shared. 'What a peculiar thing!' said the squirrel. 'We'd better go round asking if any one has seen our nuts!'

There was only one person who could tell them and that was the little mouse hidden down his hole, with a lovely pile of nuts. But did he say a word? Not he!

They Really Were Sorry

'Johnny, will you go down to the shops this morning and fetch me two bundles of sticks for lighting the fire?' said Mother. 'I haven't any left for tomorrow morning.'

'Oh bother!' said Johnny. 'My bike's gone wrong again, and I shall have to walk! It's such a long way.'

'Nonsense!' said his mother. 'Why, if I told you to go and buy ice-creams, you'd think it was no way at all! Now please don't forget, Johnny.'

Then Mother called to Jenny. 'Jenny dear – will you do something for me too? I'm so busy this morning. Will you go and buy some flowers for me at the flower-shop? Granny is coming to stay tonight and I want a nice vase of flowers for her bedroom. There are hardly any left in the garden.'

'Well, I was going to clean out my doll's house this morning,' said Jenny.

'You'll have plenty of time for that,' said her mother. 'Now do remember to get the flowers. I'll leave five pounds on the mantelpiece, look. Get some roses if you can, Granny loves those.'

Well, will you believe it, Johnny forgot all about fetching the bundles of wood that morning – and Jenny was so busy with her doll's house that when she looked at the clock she found it was too late to go to the flower-shop before dinner!

'Bother!' she said. 'Look at the time, Johnny. You haven't been to get the

firewood, and I didn't go to the flower-shop. Now there isn't time.'

'We'll go this afternoon,' said Johnny. 'It won't matter.'

But it did matter! You see, the shops closed early that day, and so it wasn't any good going shopping in the afternoon!

Mother was very cross when she found out at dinner-time that neither of the twins had done what they had promised her.

'I really thought you loved me enough to help me in little things like this,' she said. 'Now I have no firewood for tomorrow's fire, and Granny will have no flowers in her bedroom.'

The twins stared at their mother's unhappy face and felt dreadful. 'We *do* love you enough to help you. You know we do,' said Jenny. 'We meant to go to the shops this afternoon, Mummy, we really did.'

'We forgot it was early-closing day,' said Johnny. 'Mummy, don't look like that. Do, do smile.'

'I don't feel like smiling,' said

Mother, and she didn't smile at the twins all through dinner-time.

'Jenny, I don't like it when Mummy's upset,' said Johnny, when they went out to play after dinner. 'We'll have to do something to make her smile at us again. I just can't bear it.'

'Nor can I,' said Jenny. 'And I don't like to think that Granny won't have any flowers to welcome her. Do you know what I'm going to do, Johnny?'

'What?' said Johnny.

'I'm going to take my basket and go into the woods and find some bright berries and autumn leaves, and I'm going to arrange them beautifully in a vase for Granny's room,' said Jenny.

'What a good idea!' said Johnny. He thought for a moment, and then smiled. 'I've got a good idea too! I'm going with you, wheeling my barrow, and I'm going to collect dry twigs and tie them into bundles for firewood! Then Mummy will have them to light the fire with tomorrow!'

'Oh Johnny, yes! What a good idea!' said Jenny. 'Come on, let's go. You

could pick up old pine-cones too,
couldn't you? They burn well.'

Mother was surprised to see the twins
setting off down the garden path with a
basket and a barrow that afternoon.
They went straight to the woods and
began to hunt for what they wanted.

'Look, scarlet hips from the wild
roses!' said Jenny, and picked a few
sprays.

'There are some lovely pink and
orange berries over there, Jenny, look!'
said Johnny, as he hunted for dry twigs.

'What are they?'

'Spindle-berries!' said Jenny in delight. 'Oh look, they are bright pink outside, and have a brilliant orange stone in the middle, Granny will love them!'

Johnny's barrow was nearly full of dry twigs. He had picked up all the longest and straightest he could find. They were dry and brittle and would burn well.

'There are some pine-trees over there,' he said. 'Let's pick up as many cones as we can.'

They picked up about twenty nice dry

cones, and put them into the barrow too. Then Jenny found some crimson leaves on the blackberry bushes and added those to her berries. The little bunch looked very pretty.

'Now we'll go home,' said Johnny. 'My barrow won't hold any more and your basket is full. Oh look – there are nuts on that hazel tree over there! Mummy loves nuts. Let's take a special present to her too – all the biggest nuts we can find.'

They got home just before tea-time, feeling very cheerful. Their mother was nowhere to be seen. Would she smile at them when she saw them – or not?

'I'm just going to tie up my twigs into neat bundles,' said Johnny. 'I think I can make about eight. And I'll put the pine-cones into a little basket.'

While he tied his bundles with a string, Jenny arranged the berries and bright leaves in a little green vase. They looked lovely.

Then she fetched a small basket from the toy-cupboard, and put the big nuts inside. She took a piece of paper and wrote on it neatly: To darling Mummy. With love from Jenny and Johnny.

Mother still hadn't come into the sitting-room, but she would when it was tea-time. 'I'm going to put my vase of berries by her place,' said Jenny, 'and the basket of nuts too.'

'And I'll put my bundles of wood and basket of cones on her chair,' said Johnny. 'Then we'd better go and wash our hands and brush our hair, Jenny.'

They went off to the bathroom. As they washed, they heard their mother going downstairs to tea. What would she say when she saw the things that the twins had left for her in the sitting-room?

'I hope she'll smile,' said Jenny. 'Mummy doesn't look like Mummy when she won't smile.'

They ran downstairs and burst into the sitting-room. Their mother was there. She turned and looked at them— and her face was one big smile!

'You darlings!' she said. 'What

They Really Were Sorry

wonderful firewood–and cones! And what a beautiful vase for Granny's room–and what lovely nuts for me!'

'You're smiling again!' said Johnny, and gave his mother such a hug that she lost her breath. 'Now everything's all right. Isn't it, Jenny?'

'Yes,' said Jenny, happily. 'Everything's just fine!'

What No Cheese!

There was once a little bird who loved cheese. He thought it was far, far nicer than butter, and if he could steal some, he would!

He flew into the grocer's shop and pecked a big hole in the cheese there.

He sat on Dame Tippy's shopping basket as she went home, and pecked a big piece out of her bit of cheese too.

And do you know, he even went into Old Man Dingle's garden and pecked the tiny bits of cheese out of the mouse-traps he had set there to catch mice who ate his peas! Wasn't he a thief?

He ate so much cheese that he grew quite yellow, and people began to call him the cheese-bird.

They thought he was a greedy little thing, and if ever he came to tea with them, they made sure not to have any cheese, for if they did he would eat up every scrap.

So, when he popped into their houses, and they offered him bread and butter, or bread and jam, he would put his head on one side, look down his beak in a very haughty manner, and say: 'What! No cheese!'

He went to tea with Dame Frilly,
and she gave him egg sandwiches.
'What! No cheese!' he cried, and
wouldn't eat a thing.

He went to supper with Dickory-
Dock, who had got a nice meal of
sardines and cocoa ready.

'What! No cheese!' cried the greedy
bird, and he wouldn't touch anything
at all.

It seemed such a waste of a meal,
because Dickory-Dock couldn't possibly eat it all himself.

One day the pixie Long-Legs gave a fine party. There were strawberries and cream, vanilla ices and lemonade, and you would have thought anyone would have been pleased, wouldn't you?

But the little yellow bird turned up his beak at everything. 'What! No cheese!' he cried again.

Long-Legs was angry. 'No,' she said, 'there isn't any cheese, you greedy little bird.'

'Who stole cheese from the grocer?

What No Cheese!

Who stole Old Man Dingle's mouse-trap cheese? Go away, you greedy thing – and don't come back here again! Sing a song about cheese if you want to – *we* shan't listen.'

So the little bird had to fly away into our world. There he found that people were as kind as could be and put out crumbs and potato and coconut and fat – but, of course, not a scrap of cheese!

And so all day long he sits on the telegraph wires, or on a high hedge,

and sings the same little song over and over again. 'Little bit of bread but no CHEESE! Little bit of bread but no CHEESE! Little bit of bread but no CHEESE!'

Have you heard him? He is singing it this summer just as usual, for I've heard him three times already today.

We call him the yellow-hammer and he is a bird rather like a sparrow, but yellow... and dear me, how he sings his little song – 'Little bit of bread but no CHEESE!' Do see if you can hear him. He sings it as plainly as anything.

Hoo-Hoo's Party

Hoo-Hoo the Owl was very hungry. He hadn't caught a mouse or a rabbit for a week, though he had tried hard every night. Whatever should he do?

He sat in his hollow tree and thought hard. Then a wonderful idea came to him.

'I will give a party,' he said to himself. 'I will ask Whiskers the mouse, Tailer the rat, Soft-Ears the rabbit, Singer the nightingale, Mowdie the mole and Frisky the squirrel. Ha ha, hoo hoo!'

So he sent out his invitations, and this is what the cards said:

Hoo-Hoo the Owl
invites
Whiskers the mouse
to a party

*on the next full moon
night in the
Hollow Tree.*

He sent the cards, each with the name of the person written on it, to Whiskers, Tailer, Soft-Ears, Singer, Mowdie and Frisky. Then he waited for the answers.

Whiskers the mouse was delighted. He had never been to a party in his life. So he accepted gratefully.

Tailer the rat was always hungry, and the thought of a party made him joyful. He thought that he would get there early and eat a lot. So he accepted too.

Soft-Ears the rabbit read his invitation over and over again, very proudly. He had only once been to a party, and it had been so lovely that he had always longed to go to another. So he accepted the invitation too, and wrote a neat little answer.

Singer the nightingale felt quite certain that she had been invited because of her lovely voice.

I expect they will ask me to sing, she thought. That will be nice, for they will all praise my beautiful voice. So she accepted too, and sent her answer along that same day.

Mowdie the mole had been to hundreds and hundreds of parties, and he felt certain that he had another one on the same night. But when he looked in his notebook to see, he found that he hadn't. So he decided that he would go, and he scribbled an answer at once.

Frisky the squirrel read Hoo-Hoo's card carefully. Then he read it again. Then he read it for a third time.

He didn't like Hoo-Hoo, and he felt quite certain that Hoo-Hoo didn't like him.

Why, then, had he been asked to Hoo-Hoo's party?

'There is something funny about this,' said Frisky, who was very wise for his age. 'I wonder who else has been asked.'

So he went round to find out, and when he heard that Whiskers the mouse, Tailer the rat, Mowdie the mole, Soft-Ears the rabbit and Singer the nightingale had been asked, he sat and thought hard again.

At last he took his fountain-pen and wrote to say that he would go.

Then he went round to all the others and said that he would call for them on the party night, and would they please be ready before the moon was up.

'But why?' they asked. 'Hoo-Hoo doesn't want us till the moon is shining.'

'Never mind,' said Frisky. 'You do as I tell you, and you will be glad afterwards.'

So on the party night everyone was ready before the moon was up. The woods were all in darkness, and Frisky went quietly round to Whiskers, Tailer, Soft-Ears, Singer and Mowdie.

'We will all go to the hollow tree and peep inside it to see what Hoo-Hoo the owl has got for the party,' said Frisky. 'But we won't go by the front way. I know a little hole at the back and we will peep in there, so that Hoo-Hoo won't see us.'

So they all set off together, and they didn't make a scrap of noise. Soon they came to the hollow tree, and Frisky led them round to the little hole at the back and they all peeped through.

Just then the moon came up, and the little guests could see inside quite plainly.

And to their very great astonishment there was nothing to eat at all!

Not a single thing! There was a big dish, quite empty, and five empty plates.

'Good gracious!' whispered Mowdie. 'This is a funny sort of party!'

'Where are all the cakes and jellies and things?'

'Shh!' said Frisky. 'Can't you hear someone coming?'

The animals all listened and looked. And whatever do you think they saw?

Why, Hoo-Hoo the owl coming into the hollow tree with four of his friends, all owls like himself!

'Sit down,' he said. 'Our dinner will be here soon. We have only got to wait! I do hope you'll enjoy the party.'

The owls all sat down and waited. The little creatures outside hardly dared to breathe. They suddenly knew what the dinner was! It was themselves!

Then one by one they crept away to their homes. Whiskers went to his hole, Tailer went to his. Soft-Ears scampered to his burrow, and Singer flew to her

bush. Mowdie went to his nest, and only Frisky was left.

He wasn't afraid of Hoo-Hoo, and he kept his eye to the hole in the tree to see what would happen. The owls waited and waited and waited, but of course

their dinner didn't come. It had all gone home long ago!

The four owls flew at Hoo-Hoo in a rage and pecked him hard till he hooted in fright. Then they flew out of the hollow tree in a temper and left Hoo-Hoo by himself.

Then Frisky called out cheekily: 'How did your party go, Hoo-Hoo? Did you have a nice time?'

He didn't wait for Hoo-Hoo to answer, not he! He fled up to the top of the tree and hid there in safety, chuckling to himself to think how angry the owl would be. So he was – and he never gave a party again in all his life!

Adventures Under the Sea

Dick was fast asleep one night when there came flying in at his bedroom window a fairy dressed in blue and green.

'Wake up, wake up!' cried the fairy.

Dick woke with a jump, and sat up.

'What do you want?' he asked.

'Are you the little boy who picked up a jellyfish that was lying in the sun and kindly put it into a pool again?' asked the fairy.

'Yes, I did, this morning,' answered Dick.

'Well, when it got back into its home, it found the King of the Sea and asked if you might, for a treat, be taken under the sea to the sea fairies' home,' said the fairy.

'Oh, I'd *love* to come!' cried Dick.

'Come down to the seashore quickly, then, just as you are,' said the fairy. 'I'll meet you there.'

Dick slipped downstairs, and was away on the beach ever so quickly. Across the water stretched a shimmering path of moonlight.

'Hold my hand,' said the sea fairy, 'and we'll run along the moon-path.'

Dick didn't think it would hold him, but it did. And off the two went, running along the bright moon-path over

the waves.

At last they stopped. 'Now,' said the fairy, 'shut your eyes while I say some magic words to make you able to go down to my home.'

Dick shut his eyes, and the fairy sang some queer-sounding words. Dick felt himself sinking down and down and down.

'Oh,' he cried, when he opened his eyes, 'what a lovely place!'

He was standing in a great blue-green hall, decorated with long streamers of waving seaweed. At one end sat Neptune, the King of the Sea, with a crown of beautiful shells.

'Welcome!' he said. 'It isn't often I have a visitor from above the sea. Would you like to see some of the wonderful things here?'

'Oh, yes please,' said Dick.

Neptune turned to the blue and green fairy. 'Pearl,' he said, 'show Dick round our sea home.'

'Come along, Dick,' said Pearl.

'Dear me!' said Dick, staring at her,

'whatever have you done with your legs, Pearl?'

'Oh, I only use legs for the land,' laughed Pearl. 'I put a tail on down here. Isn't it a nice one?' and off she swam, with Dick following.

They came to a dark, quiet cave, in which sat a solemn little merman with a long yellow tail. He had a silvery net, and was gazing up through the water.

'What's he doing?' asked Dick.

'Look up,' said Pearl. 'Can you see those shining things right up there on

the top of the water?'

'Yes,' said Dick. 'They're stars reflected in the sea, aren't they?'

'Yes! Watch,' said Pearl.

The merman suddenly flung his net up into the water. It rose up and up. When he pulled it down again Dick saw it was full of faint shining stars.

'He caught the stars you saw reflected on the top of the water,' said Pearl.

The merman picked out the smallest, and threaded them on a fine string.

'They're for the baby sea fairies to play with,' he said. 'The rest I throw away; they're too big.'

He threw a lot down on the ground. To Dick's surprise they turned pink and slowly moved away.

'Goodness me,' he cried, 'they've turned into starfish!'

'Yes, they always do that,' answered Pearl. 'Now you know why they're shaped like stars. Come along!'

She took him out into a wide, open, sandy place, with rocks all around and beautiful sea flowers. Playing about were baby sea fairies, all with tails.

'Would you like to see them play their favourite game?'

'Yes, I would,' answered Dick.

Pearl went to a big square rock and opened the top, just like a box-lid. All the baby fairies swam over to her, calling out:

'Our balloons, our balloons!'

'Oh, you're giving them jellyfish!' cried Dick in surprise.

'Yes, they're not like *your* balloons,' laughed Pearl, 'and they're made of jelly, so that they don't burst and frighten the babies.'

Dick watched the little fairies. Each held on to the streamers hanging down from the jellyfish, and away they floated, up and up, carried by their strange balloons.

'Oh,' cried a baby, tumbling down, 'mine is broken!' His jellyfish went sailing away by itself. Soon three or four more babies came tumbling down, laughing and rolling on the sand.

'There go their balloons!' cried Dick.
'Yes,' said Pearl, 'and I expect you'll
find them floating about helplessly
somewhere at the edge of the sea
tomorrow, with their strings hanging
down.'

'I often wondered what use jellyfish were,' said Dick. 'I'm so glad I know now.'

'Now we'll go and see the white horses,' said Pearl, swimming off.

'Oh, are there *really* white horses in the sea?' asked Dick. 'I thought they were just white foam on the top of waves.'

'Dear me, no!' said Pearl. 'When they gallop along under the sea, and make big waves come, it's their curly white manes you can see peeping up here and there – not just white foam!'

'Oh, there they are!' cried Dick. There in front of him stretched a wide field of green seaweed, and munching it were great white horses with beautiful curly manes of snow-white.

'Stroke one,' said Pearl; 'they're quite tame.'

Dick stroked one, and it felt as soft as foam.

'I'm going to let one take you home,' said Pearl. 'Jump on his back.'

Dick climbed up.

'Goodbye!' called Pearl. 'I'm glad you came.'

'Goodbye!' shouted Dick, holding on to the thick mane of his horse as it galloped off.

When it got to the seashore it stood still. Dick slipped off and watched it disappear into the waves.

'*What* a lovely night I've had!' he said, as he ran back home again and cuddled down into bed.

Tarrydiddle Town

Sarah lived with her mother and father right on the edge of a magic wood. Her mother often warned her not to go wandering too far into the wood, in case she disturbed the fairy folk, and made them cross.

'I *should* like to follow that little twisty path under the oak trees,' said Sarah to her mother one day.

'Hush, child! Never think of such a thing!' said her mother sharply. 'And you must keep indoors with me today and help me make the bread.'

Sarah pouted and sulked. She was a dreadfully lazy little girl, and she didn't want to stay indoors at all. So when her mother was not looking she slipped out and ran into the wood.

'I *will* follow that little twisty path!' she said to herself.

She ran down the little path under the big oak trees. It became darker and darker, for the wood grew thick and kept out the sunshine.

Suddenly Sarah heard voices, and crept behind a tree, a little afraid.

'The king says we *must* be cleaner and tidier,' said a voice crossly. 'I can't think how we're going to manage it!'

'If only we could find a servant,' sighed another voice; 'but nobody ever comes to Tarrydiddle Town.'

Just then a twig that Sarah was treading on suddenly snapped with a loud noise.

'Someone's there!' cried the voices, and Sarah heard rushing feet.

Then two strange-looking creatures appeared in front of her, and seized hold of her wrists. They had big heads with very thick hair, long noses, and wide mouths. Their bodies were small and their feet large.

'Who are you,' cried one creature,

'and what are you doing in our part of the wood?'

'I'm Sarah,' said Sarah; 'and do let me go, you're hurting.'

'Can you sweep?' suddenly asked the other creature.

'Yes,' answered Sarah.

'And clean windows, and make beds?'

'Oh yes, yes!' said Sarah crossly; 'but why are you asking me such silly questions?'

'Splendid!' cried both creatures.

'We'll have you for a servant! Come along with us!' and they dragged Sarah off.

'Where are you taking me to?' asked Sarah.

'To Tarrydiddle Town,' they answered. 'The King of Fairyland visited us the other day, and said our town was so dreadfully untidy and dirty that if we didn't make it better he would punish us. But it's been untidy for so long that we've forgotten how to make it bright and clean.'

'Well, I'd like to visit Tarrydiddle Town,' said Sarah, 'but I'm not going to be your servant, so there!'

'We have cream cakes and treacle pudding at every meal,' said one Tarrydiddle.

'Oh!' said Sarah, 'I'd love to go to your town. Let's hurry up and go!'

When the Tarrydiddles saw that Sarah was eager to go with them they were very pleased. They hurried along until they came to a little stream, on which rocked a canoe.

'Jump in!' cried the two queer creatures to Sarah. She jumped in, and off
went the boat down the stream with
the three of them.

The stream soon left the wood, and
came out into open fields. Presently,

away in the distance, Sarah saw the
queerest village that ever was built.

The houses, all of them small, were
higgledypiggledy and crooked. The
chimneys were not only on the roofs,
but sometimes stuck out of the walls.
Some of the houses had doors very high

up, but with no steps up to them. Sarah wondered however the people got into them.

'Here we are!' said the Tarrydiddles, jumping out. Sarah jumped out too.

'Well!' she said, as she came near the town. 'Well, I never saw such a queer, untidy, dirty place in my life! Just *look* at the windows! They're thick with dirt! And the window-sills! Absolutely black!'

Sarah wandered round Tarrydiddle town for a good while. The streets were crooked and wanted sweeping, for there were all sorts of papers flying about.

'I'll peep into a few houses now,' said Sarah. She walked into one, and found the floor dirty with mud. There was dust on everything, and all the curtains wanted washing.

'Ugh!' said Sarah, walking out. 'What a horrid place Tarrydiddle Town is! I shan't stay *here* long!'

Soon she came to a street of shops, and to her delight there were rows and

rows of cream cakes and big plates of steaming hot treacle pudding.

'You can go and have anything in the shop you like!' one of the Tarrydiddles told her. 'We don't pay for anything here.'

Sarah ran in, and ate five cream cakes and two plates of treacle pudding! At the end she said, 'Now I want to go home, please.'

'Oh no, you can't,' said the Tarrydiddles. 'You must stop and work for us, and show us how to make our town clean.'

Sarah stamped and roared and frowned and sulked, but it was all no use. The lazy little girl had to do what she was told. She was taken to the biggest house in the town and told to put it straight. How she wished she had stayed at home and helped her mother!

'Well, I'll try to clean the house,' said Sarah tearfully; 'but will you let me go home afterwards?'

'You must stay here a week,' said the Tarrydiddles, 'for the king is coming then. If he says our town is tidy and clean we'll let you go home. If not, you must stay till the king comes again, and that may not be for months and months.'

'Only a week!' exclaimed Sarah. 'Why, I can't possibly get things clean and tidy in a week! You are *horrid*, you Tarrydiddles!'

Sarah began working as quickly as she could. She *was* so afraid the king would come and say Tarrydiddle Town was untidy, and then she wouldn't be able to go home.

'I'll scrub all the floors,' said Sarah to herself. So she got a pail of water, and scrubbed the floors of the little house till they shone.

'How clever! How beautiful!' said all the Tarrydiddles, watching. And they ran straight home and scrubbed all *their* floors to see if they could make them shine too.

Then Sarah dusted all the walls and all the furniture, and polished it till she could see herself in the table and chair legs.

'How wonderful!' exclaimed the Tarrydiddles, and off they all went to do the same.

The next day Sarah pulled down all the curtains and tablecloths, and washed them all as white as snow in a big wash-tub of hot water. They looked simply lovely all hanging out on the line to dry.

All Tarrydiddle Town was busy washing too, and copying Sarah.

'How clever you are! How clever!' they kept saying to Sarah, who was beginning to feel rather pleased with the way the house looked.

All through the week Sarah could find nothing to eat but cream cakes and treacle pudding. At last she grew so tired of them that she could hardly bear to look at them.

'Oh, if only I could taste some of mother's home-made bread!' she sighed. 'Oh, I *do* hope the king will think things are tidy, and I can go home!'

She cleaned the windows, and whitened the window-sills, and blacked the grates.

'Beautiful! Wonderful!' said all the funny little Tarrydiddles, going off to do the same in their own houses.

Then came the last day. Sarah looked all over the house, and could find nothing dirty, and nothing untidy. Everything shone and glittered.

Tomorrow the king is coming, she thought. I must bake some bread, and get the streets cleaned today, and then that's really all!

She caught up a broom, and hurried outside.

'Clever girl! Marvellous girl!' cried the Tarrydiddles, watching her. 'Why didn't *we* think of sweeping the streets?' And soon all of them were sweeping too, and the streets were as clean as clean.

Sarah made some bread after that, as she thought the king might like something else to eat besides the ever-lasting cream cakes and treacle pud-

ding. After that she was so tired that
she dropped asleep in the kitchen.

'Oh, how lovely everything looks!'
she cried next morning as she went
round the town, and saw all the houses
clean and tidy and neat, like the one
she herself had lived in. 'There's only

one thing left to do!'

'What's that?' cried the Tarry-diddles, crowding round her.

'Wash yourselves, and brush your hair,' said Sarah. They all went off to do it.

Tara! Tan-tan-tara! Tara!

'The king! The king!' shouted all the Tarrydiddles, rushing out clean and tidy to meet the king and his courtiers. Sarah went too.

'Greetings to you, people of Tarry-diddle Town,' said the grand king of Fairyland. And then his majesty went into every house to see it if were tidy and clean.

'Splendid! Marvellous!' cried the king, as he went into one after another. 'Who has helped you to do all this?'

'Sarah has! Sarah has!' shouted the Tarrydiddles, dragging her forward.

'You have done splendid work,' said the king. 'I will grant you a wish. What would you like?'

'Oh, may I go home again, please?'

begged Sarah. 'I'm so tired of cream cakes and treacle pudding, and I can only bake bread myself. I'll never be lazy again.'

'Yes, you may go home,' said the king kindly; 'and if Tarrydiddle Town ever gets dirty again, I shall know whom to send for to put it right, shan't I, Tarrydiddles? So be careful to keep your houses spick and span in future!'

He waved his wand. A great wind rushed round Sarah and carried her away. Then *bump*! she was standing on the ground again in front of her mother's cottage.

'Mother! Mother!' called Sarah, rushing in. 'I've come home, and I'll never be lazy again.'

And if you ever meet a little girl who can't bear to eat cream cakes or treacle pudding, ask if her name is Sarah, and whether she has heard anything more of Tarrydiddle Town.

Gillian and the Lamb

Once upon a time Gillian went down to the farm to fetch some eggs all by herself.

'I shall take my doll Betty with me,' she said to her mother. 'She has had a bad cold, and the sunny air will do her good. I shan't be long, Mummy.'

So Gillian tucked her doll up well, put her purse with the egg-money under the cover of the pram, and set out down the lane, feeling rather proud to think she was out by herself.

She went over the bridge and peeped at the brown stream underneath. She saw a great many white daisies in the grass, and some early buttercups. She heard a lark singing so high up in the sky that she couldn't see him at all.

'I hope you are enjoying this nice walk,' she said to Betty, her doll, who was sitting up with her woolly hat on her curly hair.

Soon Gillian came to the farm. There were so many hens running about that she had to be quite careful where she wheeled her doll's pram. They said 'Cluck, cluck!' to her in loud, cheerful voices, and she said 'Cluck cluck!' back. It was easy to talk hen-language.

She wheeled her pram up to the farm door. She knocked. Nobody came. She knocked again, a bit harder this time. Still nobody came.

'Oh dear!' said Gillian. 'That means no one is in – and I shall have to go home without the eggs. What a pity!'

So she set off home again. She had just passed the field where the big haystack stood when she saw something moving in the hedge. She stopped to see what it was.

'Oh, it's a tiny baby lamb!' said Gillian, in surprise. 'It's escaped from the field. Go back, lamb! If you don't, a car may come along and knock you down.'

But the lamb wouldn't go back. It came limping over to Gillian, and then she saw that it had torn its leg on the barbed wire that ran along the hedges there. She knelt down and looked at the leg.

'When I hurt my leg I have it bathed and some good stuff put on it,' said Gillian. 'Your mother sheep can't do that – but perhaps she will lick it better if you go back to her. Look – there she is, peeping through the hedge at you!'

Sure enough there was a big mother sheep putting her head through the hole in the hedge, baa-ing loudly. Gillian picked up the tiny lamb and carried it back to the hole – but it wouldn't go through it! It kept limping back to Gillian.

'Whatever shall I do with you, lamb?' she said. 'I can't leave you here in the lane. And you won't go back to your mother. And there is no one at the farm this morning to look after you.'

She stared at the lamb and the lamb stared back at Gillian, 'Maa-aa-aa!' said the lamb, in a small, high voice, and it wriggled its tail like a hazel catkin on the hedge.

'I shall take you home to my own mother,' said Gillian. 'She is kind and will know what to do with you. She will make your leg better.'

'Maa-aa-aa!' said the lamb.

'Come along then,' said Gillian. 'Walk close behind me, lamb.' But the lamb wouldn't. It just stood there in the middle of the lane, maa-ing and wriggling its tail.

'Well, really, I don't know what to do with you!' said Gillian. And then an idea came into her head. Of course! She could wheel the lamb in her pram! It was quite small enough to go in.

So she picked up the tiny lamb, and put it gently in the pram beside Betty, the doll. 'I'm afraid you will be a bit squashed, Betty,' said Gillian. 'But I can't help it. Lie down, lamb. I'll cover you up nicely.'

The lamb was surprised to find himself in a pram. He lay quite still. Gillian covered him up. She tucked him in well in case he wriggled loose. 'Maa-aa-aa!' said the lamb, and he sniffed at Betty, the doll.

Gillian wheeled the pram up the lane. She met Mr Logs, the woodman. 'Good morning,' he said. 'And how's your doll today?'

'She's a bit squashed because she's sharing the pram with a lamb,' said Gillian. Mr Logs bent to see – and

when he saw the little lamb looking at him, how he laughed!

'That's a funny sight!' he said. 'Well, well, well!'

Then Gillian met Mrs Thimble, who did sewing for lots of people. 'Good morning, Gillian,' she said. 'And how's your doll today?'

'She's a bit squashed because she's sharing the pram with a lamb,' said Gillian. Mrs Thimble bent down to see, and how she laughed when the little lamb said 'Maa-aa-aa!' to her.

'No, *I'm* not your ma-aa-aa!' she said. 'I can hear your ma baa-ing for you in the field!'

'Oh, there's my mummy!' said Gillian. 'I must go and show her my lamb. Goodbye!'

She wheeled the pram in at the gate of Old Thatch. Her mother was weeding a bed nearby. She called her.

'Mummy! Here's a lamb with a hurt leg! It wouldn't go back into its field — and there's no one at the farm — so I've brought it home for you to mend.'

Her mother stood up in astonishment and looked for the lamb. She didn't think of looking into the pram!

'Where *is* the lamb?' she said.

'Maa-aa-aa!' said the lamb, waving one of its feet over the pram cover. How Gillian's mother laughed! She laughed and she laughed to see the lamb lying in the pram with Betty, the doll.

'Whatever will you do next, Gillian?' she said. She took the lamb out of the pram and looked at its leg.

'Go and get me a basin of water,' she

said. So Gillian ran off. Very soon the lamb's leg was washed and some good stuff put on it. It wasn't very bad. It didn't even need a bandage, though Gillian badly wanted to put one on.

Just then the farmer's wife came by the gate, home from shopping, and she looked in. How surprised she was to see the lamb in the garden of Old Thatch!

Gillian told her all about it, and the farmer's wife laughed when she heard about the lamb being wheeled in the pram.

'Thank you for being so kind as to look after it for me,' she said to Gillian. 'I'll carry it back to the field now, and mend the fence.'

So she did – but always after that, when Gillian went down the lane the little lamb watched for her and maa-ed to her. It put its tiny head through the hedge, and you may be sure that Gillian always stopped to rub its little black nose!

'I'm Going Away!'

'I'm going away!' said the monkey, looking very cross. 'Right away. And I'll never come back!'

'Don't be silly,' said the teddy-bear. 'Just because we won't let you tease the little clockwork mouse, or put beads down the dolls' house chimney, or pull the toy elephant by his trunk!'

'You're always telling me not to do things!' said the monkey fiercely. 'Interfering! Saying "Don't!" Calling out "No, no!" I'm tired of it. I'm going away.'

'Let him go, Teddy,' said the rocking-horse. 'We're all tired of him. It will be very, very peaceful without Monkey. Goodbye, Monkey! Happy journey!'

'I haven't gone yet,' said the monkey.

'I must pack my bag.'

He found his little bag and packed it with his spare coat and tie, and a tiny brush and comb. Then he put it on his shoulder and stared round at the toys.

'Well – I'm off!' he said. 'I shall find some nicer people to live with. People who don't say "No!" and "Don't!" Goodbye!'

'Goodbye,' said everyone. 'Send us a postcard when you get there.'

'I shan't,' said Monkey, and off he went out of the door.

He was soon out in the garden, and then he ran out of the back gate into the lane. He walked along, his bag on his shoulder. Now to find some really nice people to live with!

He came to a rabbit-burrow and saw a baby rabbit sitting outside. Ah – perhaps the rabbits would like him to live with them!

'Good morning,' said Monkey. 'May I come and live with you?'

'Certainly,' said the little rabbit. 'Follow me.' And he turned and ran into the hole behind him. Monkey followed, knocking his head against the top of the burrow, and finding everything very dark.

'Wait a bit!' he called to the rabbit. 'It's so dark, I can't see. Where's a

light?'

'We haven't one,' said the rabbit in surprise. 'We live down in the dark.'

'Oh, how dreadful!' said the monkey, thinking of the nice bright playroom where he and the other toys lived. 'I can't live *here*! I'll go back.'

So back he went and came out of the dark burrow. On he walked, bag on shoulder. He soon came to a field where a small pony stood. 'Hrrrrumph!' said the pony in surprise. 'What kind of animal are you?'

'I'm a toy,' said Monkey. 'You look nice. I think I'll come and live with you. Where's your home?'

'I'll show you,' said the pony and trotted off to his stables. 'I live here at night. Look – you could make a nice warm bed for yourself in one of these mangers full of hay.'

'I will,' said Monkey and climbed up to one. Certainly the hay was very soft and smelt sweet. He was tired and cuddled down. He fell asleep.

But he soon woke up again! Something was breathing over him. Something was nosing strongly into the hay. Someone seemed to be trying to nibble him!

Monkey leapt out at once. He saw a big grey horse looking at him in astonishment. 'Hrrrrumph!' said the

horse, in surprise. 'What are you doing in my hay? I nearly ate you!'

'Stupid creature!' said Monkey, and ran out of the stables, really scared. He put his bag on his shoulder and set off once more.

Soon he met a puppy-dog, who ran up to him, wagging his tail. 'Woof!' said the puppy. 'Play with me! Do play with me. I'm lonely.'

'Right!' said Monkey, proudly. Ah, here was someone who wanted him – someone who wouldn't say 'Don't', and stop him from doing what he wanted.

The puppy pranced round the monkey and played 'catch' and really made him feel very tired. 'I must have a rest,' said Monkey. 'Where do you live?'

'In that little wooden house over there,' said the puppy, nodding his head at a nice kennel nearby. 'I share it with my big brother.'

Monkey ran to it and went inside. It was full of straw and had rather a peculiar smell. But Monkey was so tired that he really couldn't bother about a smell. He was just creeping into the straw when a loud sound made him jump.

'GRRRRRRR!' What a growl he heard, just behind him! Monkey turned round and saw a big dog – the puppy's brother. He was growling and showing his teeth.

'Don't do that!' said Monkey. 'I'm a friend of your brother's. I've come to live here with you.'

'Grrrr!' said the big dog again. '*I* know what you're after! You're hunting for the bone I buried in the straw. Grrr! I'll pounce on you for that.'

'Don't be silly!' cried the monkey in fright. 'As if I want a silly, smelly bone!'

'My bone isn't silly, and it has a very *fine* smell!' said the big dog, angrily. 'Come out!'

He pounced on the scared monkey and pulled him out by his coat and trousers. There was a loud tearing noise.

'You've torn my coat – and made a hole in my trousers!' shouted the

monkey. 'Bad dog! I won't live with *you*. Or your smelly bone either!'

And he ran at top speed down the path and into the lane. The dog ran after him, growling. Monkey ran and ran and ran – he ran long after the dog had given up the chase. Then he sat down under a bush and cried.

'Nobody wants me! I've torn my coat and trousers! I've left my little bag behind in that kennel. Oh, why did I run away from dear old Teddy and the kind rocking-horse and the pretty little

dolls in the playroom? Boo-hoo-hoo –
I'm VERY unhappy!'

A little voice called to him from the
window of the house whose garden he
was sitting in. 'Hey there! Who's
crying? Can we help you?'

Monkey stood up at once, in great
surprise. 'Why – that's Teddy-Bear's
voice, I know it is! Goodness me, I ran
miles away – and then ran miles back
again to my very own house! Teddy, it's
me, Monkey!'

'Oh! Well, come back!' said Teddy,

waving a fat paw from the window. 'We've missed you already.'

'And I've missed *you*!' cried Monkey, running to the window. 'Nobody wants me. I've been down a horrid dark burrow, and nearly eaten by a horse, and almost gobbled by a horrid dog. I want to come home again.'

Well, he went back to the playroom, of course, and everyone was kind to him. How glad he was to see the bright, cheerful playroom again, and the faces of his friends.

'I'll never be bad again,' he said. But, of course, he *is* sometimes naughty — and then Teddy looks at him and says: 'Go and pack your bag, Monkey. Run away again. Hurry now!'

But Monkey never does. 'Please, I'm sorry,' he says. 'I'm sorry, I'm sorry! I won't ever run away again. East, west, home's best! I'll *never* run away again!'

Who was the Nibbler?

Once, when the children had had a party, somebody knocked two sugar biscuits down on the floor. Nobody saw them fall, so nobody picked them up.

And that night, when the children were fast asleep, Rosebud, the doll with curly golden hair, slipped out of her cot and picked them up. The toys crowded round her.

'Break them up and give each of us a bit,' said the monkey.

'Certainly not. They belong to the children!' said Rosebud, shocked. 'I shall put them on this little chair, and perhaps the children will see them in the morning.'

So she put them there and left them. All the toys went back to the toy cupboard to sleep.

But in the middle of the night the big fat teddy-bear got up and peeped out of the cupboard. Nobody was about. The moon shone in at the window, and he could quite clearly see those two biscuits sitting on the little chair.

'I *must* have a nibble,' he said to himself. 'I must! Nobody will know!'

He went over to the chair – and just as he got there he heard a little sound behind him. It was Whiskers, the mouse who lived in a hole behind the wall.

'I smelt them too,' said Whiskers. 'Whose are they?'

'The children dropped them at tea-time,' said Teddy. 'You're not to have any, I was here first!'

'If they belong to the children, I wouldn't *dream* of having any!' said Whiskers, and went back to his hole.

Teddy took a nibble at one biscuit. It was delicious. He nibbled it all round, and then he couldn't eat any more. As he went back to the toy cupboard, he saw Whiskers' nose sticking out of his hole. He was watching the bear.

'You're a mean, horrid thing!' squeaked Whiskers, and ran down his hole when the bear came over to him.

Next day the toys were cross to find that one biscuit had been nibbled all round. 'Who did it?' they said.

'Whiskers the mouse,' said the bear at once. 'Look at the nibbles – they're a mouse's.'

What a dreadful story to tell! And the worst of it was that the toys believed him. They went to the mouse's hole and called Whiskers some horrid names:

'Nasty little nibbler!'

'Horrid little thief!'

'Wicked little mouse!'

Whiskers was very upset and stayed at the bottom of his hole. But when everything was quiet the next night, he scampered up again and peeped out of his hole. Aha! There was that bad teddy-bear nibbling at the *second* biscuit!

The bear saw him watching and ran

to the hole. 'Stop watching me!' he growled. 'I won't have it!'

'I'll tell the toys about you!' squeaked Whiskers. 'I will, I will!'

'You won't! I won't let you watch me, and I won't let you come out of your hole!' said Teddy. He went across to the corner where the big box of bricks stood, and carried it to the mouse's hole. He put the box down just in front of it.

'There! Now you can't peep or come out!' he said. 'It serves you right, I shall tell all the other toys it was *you* that nibbled the biscuits! Horrid little mouse!'

The bear couldn't eat any more biscuit that night, and he went back to the cupboard. In the morning the toys were very angry to see that the second biscuit was now nibbled all round the edges!

'Look at that! Whiskers must have come and nibbled this second biscuit!' said Rosebud. 'It's too bad of him. We'll go and call him names again.'

'I've put the box of bricks in front of his hole,' said the bear. 'He won't come out again and do any nibbling!'

'How clever of you, Teddy,' said the toys.

'I do hope the children will soon come and find the biscuits,' said the monkey. 'They don't look very nice now.'

Now, the next night the teddy-bear was glad to think that Whiskers the mouse couldn't watch him. He tip-toed to the nibbled biscuits, and began to nibble all round the first one again.

Delicious!

Somebody crept into the nursery, somebody very small and quiet. The somebody ran like a shadow to the toy cupboard and woke up the monkey. He woke up Rosebud too, and the sailor doll. He whispered in their ears:

'Wake up! Peep out of the cupboard. See who is nibbling the biscuits!'

And the monkey, Rosebud, and the sailor doll all peeped out. There, right in the bright moonlight, was the fat teddy-bear. Nibble, nibble, nibble!

'Oh!' shouted the monkey, making the bear jump almost out of his skin. 'So it's YOU! And you said it was Whiskers the mouse. You bad, horrid bear!'

And then Rosebud, the monkey, and the sailor doll chased the bear round the nursery with Rosebud's umbrella – and how they spanked him when they caught him.

'Who told you?' wept the bear.

'Whiskers,' said Rosebud. 'Poor little Whiskers! You made us call him such horrid names too!'

Who was the Nibbler?

'He *couldn't* have told you,' wept the bear. 'I blocked up his hole with the brick-box. He couldn't get out.'

'But he's here – look!' said Rosebud. And sure enough Whiskers ran out from behind her, his nose twitching up and down.

'How did you get here? Your hole is still blocked up!' said the bear, wiping his eyes.

'Oh, I've another hole, silly – over there!' said the mouse. 'I just came up through that one. Aha! I watched you again – and I went and woke the others. It serves you right.'

'What's to happen to the biscuits?' said the monkey. 'They look simply horrid now. We'd better throw them away.'

'Couldn't *I* have them?' begged the little mouse. 'I'm so hungry, I haven't had anything to eat today.'

'Yes, of course – *you* shall eat them!' said Rosebud. 'Here you are, Whiskers – and we're very, very sorry we called you such horrid names.'

Whiskers took the biscuits and ran to his second hole, just near the fireplace. Well, well – who would have thought of him having another hole!

'He deserves the biscuits,' said Rosebud. 'As for you, Teddy, you'll have to be good for a long, long time before we forget about tonight!'

Well – they've *almost* forgotten by now, so I suppose the bear has somehow managed to be good for weeks and weeks. As for Whiskers, he's a very fat little mouse indeed. He *did* enjoy those biscuits!

A Lovely Welcome Home

Once upon a time the Fairy Queen had worked so hard that the king had to take her away to stay by the Dream Sea. She was so dreadfully tired that he kept her there all the summer.

'But what will all my fairies do without me to help them?' she kept saying.

'Never mind that,' said the king. 'They must get on somehow or other, and you must have a long rest.'

Of course all the fairies in Fairyland missed her very much. It seemed very strange not to have someone in the palace who was always ready to listen to them, or to see what work they were doing.

'When is our queen coming back?' they asked the palace fairies.

'She is coming back in *two* weeks,' they answered joyfully. 'We had a letter this morning, brought by a peacock butterfly.'

'Hurray! hurray!' shouted the fairies, and they flew off all over Fairyland, as fast as they could, to spread the good news.

'We must do something lovely to welcome her home again,' said the chief fairies. 'We'll hold a great meeting about it.'

So a meeting was held in the biggest hall of the palace, and hundreds and hundreds of fairies came.

'The queen is coming home through the green beech wood, along the blackberry lanes, through the dewy field, and then up the palace gardens,' said the Lord High Chamberlain of Fairyland.

'We will polish all our dewdrops most beautifully, and hang them on the grasses,' said the fairies who lived in the dewy field.

'And we'll go and ask the blackberries to grow very black and sweet, so that when the queen comes along she may pick some for herself,' cried the lane fairies, flying off at once.

'The rose trees will grow their very best roses,' said the palace gardeners joyfully, 'and perhaps the dear queen will pick one for her buttonhole.'

'See that a glorious supper is prepared for her Majesty,' commanded the Lord High Chamberlain, turning to the fairy cooks.

'Oh yes, yes, yes!' cried the cooks. 'We'll make a big sugar cake, shaped just like a castle, and a pudding with jam on top and ice-cream underneath!'

Only the wood fairies said nothing.

'What will *you* do to welcome back the queen?' asked the Lord High Chamberlain.

'We don't know,' they answered sadly. 'The trees have lost their beautiful fresh spring green, and they look tired and dark, now it's autumn.'

'Couldn't you brighten them up a bit?' asked the chamberlain. 'Why don't you hang some flags on them?'

'Oh, they wouldn't like that,' said the wood fairies. 'But we'll go and ask them.'

Off they flew to the beech wood.

They told the trees that the queen was coming home in two weeks, and made them most excited about it. They waved their branches about as they talked.

'What *can* we do to welcome her back?' they asked.

'I've got an idea,' suddenly said a

wood fairy, 'but I don't know if you'd like it.'

'Tell us,' begged the beech trees.

'Well, you're dusty and dark green now,' said the fairy, 'but if you'd let us paint you a gay colour, you'd look lovely.'

'Oh, do, do,' said all the trees.

'Oh, I don't think we could do that,' said the chief fairy. 'The paint would make your leaves look lovely, but it might kill them too, and make them drop off.'

'We wouldn't mind, even if it hurt us,' said all the trees. 'We love the queen, and we'd do anything to make things beautiful when she came home.'

'All right,' answered the wood fairies. 'We'll go and get some gold-brown paint for you.'

They flew off at once and mixed some beautiful gold-brown paint. They told the lane fairies what they were going to do with it.

'What a splendid idea!' they said. 'We'll ask the blackberries if they'd like their leaves painted red. We are sure they would.'

The idea spread all through the woods and lanes and hedges. The wood fairies were very busy. They sat up in the beech trees and painted every leaf a lovely golden brown. The lane fairies made the blackberry brambles perfectly beautiful with red leaves – and all the other trees, oak, hawthorn, and elm, begged to be painted too.

On the day that the queen was expected home, Fairyland looked simply glorious. The beech wood was a waving glory of gold; the other trees shone red, brown, or yellow; and as for the creeper over the palace wall, well, it almost made you blink to look at it, it was such a brilliant red!

As the queen journeyed home she could hardly believe her eyes!

'What *has* happened to all the trees?' she cried. 'How beautiful they are! What *have* the wood fairies been doing?'

'They've painted our leaves,' whispered the trees proudly.

172

'But that will soon make your leaves fall off,' said the queen.

'They'll grow again in the spring,' answered the trees, as one of the gold-brown leaves fluttered down for the queen to tread on. 'And *we* don't mind, if only you're pleased and happy.'

'Oh, it's a *lovely* homecoming!' cried the queen, 'and everything does look so wonderfully beautiful. Don't you think we could always make things look like this in the autumn?'

'Yes, let's,' cried all the fairies, and all the trees. 'We'd *love* to!'

So every year now, directly the autumn comes, the beeches and the blackberry bushes, the oaks and the creepers, are all painted in gold and brown, red, yellow, and orange, just as they were ages ago when the Fairy Queen was welcomed home from the Dream Sea.

The Tale of Kimmy-Cat

There was once a cat called Kimmy-Cat who loved going fishing. He fished in his master's goldfish bowl and caught six little goldfish and ate them. He was smacked for that, but *he* didn't care! He just waited till more fish were put in the bowl and then he fished for those and ate them too!

Then he found his way to the neighbour's pond, and waited patiently by the water until a very big and beautiful fish came by. Out went Kimmy-Cat's paw, and the poor fish was caught and eaten.

Kimmy got into trouble for that, and he was well smacked. The other cats laughed at him.

'Fancy going fishing!' they said. 'You

are a silly, Kimmy-Cat! Why, you have nice fresh codfish cooked for you every day, and yet you go catching those poor goldfish. We think you are a naughty cat.'

'Goldfish taste so nice,' said Kimmy-Cat. 'You just come with me and taste them.'

But none of the other cats would do such a naughty thing. So Kimmy-Cat had to go alone. He didn't dare to go to the pond next door, so he roamed away by himself to look for another one.

Soon he came to a wood, and right in the very middle of it he found a perfectly round pond with pink water-lilies growing on the surface.

But better than water-lilies to Kimmy-Cat was a big fish, very golden, and with bright diamond-like eyes. It swam slowly about the little pond, and shone like gold.

'Ho!' said Kimmy-Cat to himself. 'That's the fish for me!'

He crouched down and waited until the fish came near the bank. Then in a

flash he shot out his paw and caught it. It landed on the bank, and wriggled to get away from him. But Kimmy-Cat got its tail into his mouth, and was just going to start eating the fish, when a voice shouted at him:

'Leave that fish alone! You wicked cat, drop that fish at once!'

Out of a little cottage came a small man in red with a pointed cap on his head. Kimmy-Cat saw that he was very tiny, so he took no notice of him. But the little man ran right up to him and took the fish away. He slipped it into the water and it swam off, none the worse for its adventure.

'You bad cat!' said the little man. 'Haven't you been taught not to go fishing? It's as bad as stealing, to go fishing in other people's ponds. That goldfish is my pet, and I've had it for twenty years.'

'I've a good mind to sit here and catch it again,' said Kimmy-Cat.

Suddenly the little man looked closely at Kimmy-Cat's tail – and then he began to laugh and dance about in glee!

'Ho, ho, ho!' he shouted. 'You've eaten a tiny bit of my fish's tail, and won't you be sorry for it! My fish is magic, and you'll be sorry you ever touched it! Ho, ho!'

Kimmy-Cat looked at his tail. Then he looked again – and, oh dear me, whatever was this! His own tail was vanishing, and he was growing a fish-tail instead!

Kimmy-Cat looked at it in horror. Even as he watched it grew bigger and

bigger. At last his own tail was com-
pletely gone – and in its place was a fine
fish-tail, golden bright and double-
pointed.

'Oh, my!' said Kimmy-Cat in dismay.
'What a dreadful thing! Here, little
man, change it back at once!'

'I can't!' said the little man, still
capering about in delight. 'No one can
take it away for you, because it's magic.
You'll have to go on wearing it – and
every fish you eat will make it grow
bigger still!'

Kimmy-Cat gave a loud miaow, and ran away in fright. This was the worst thing that had ever happened to him! He ran all the way home and curled himself up in his basket before any of the other cats could see him.

But they smelt his fish-tail, and came crowding round him, thinking he had got a fish in his basket. The dogs came too, and so did the cook.

'Have you got a fish there?' she said sharply. 'You know that the master forbade you to go fishing any more, you naughty cat. Get up and let me see if you have a fish!'

But Kimmy-Cat wouldn't move. He didn't want anyone to see his fish-tail. The cook suddenly became cross, tipped him out of his basket – and then stared in the greatest surprise at his tail!

'Good gracious, what's this!' she cried. 'Why, what have you done to your tail, Kimmy? It's a fish-tail!'

All the cats and dogs sniffed at it, and then they began to laugh.

The Tale of Kimmy-Cat

'Ho, Kimmy's turning into a fish because he catches so many!' they said. 'Look at his tail! He's half a fish!'

Kimmy-Cat went very red indeed. He curled up in his basket again, and pretended to take no notice. But soon more cats came up and more still, all attracted by the fishy smell in Kimmy-Cat's basket. In despair Kimmy-Cat jumped out and ran away.

But that was no use either – for wherever he went the cats nearby smelt fish and ran after him. How Kimmy-Cat wished he had never gone fishing!

At last he went back to the little man and begged for his help.

'I couldn't help you even if I wanted to, which I don't,' said the little man. 'The best thing you can do is to hide away until your own tail has grown again. It will take about a month, I should think.'

'But where can I hide?' asked poor Kimmy-Cat.

'Well, you can hide in my little house here, if you like,' said the man. 'But in return for that you must do all the work in my house for me. That will be very good for you, for I can see that you have thought of nothing and nobody but yourself up till now. You are too fat, besides being disobedient and unkind.'

Kimmy-Cat said nothing. He at once went indoors and found an apron to put on. Then he took a broom and began to work hard.

His own tail began to grow again. It gradually pushed the fish-tail away, and at last, by the time the month was nearly up, there was nothing left of the fish-tail except for a tiny spike at the end of his own furry tail.

Kimmy-Cat was so glad. He had learnt a lot. He was a different cat when he said goodbye to the little man and went home again.

'Here comes Kimmy!' cried all the other animals. 'Where have you been, Kimmy-Cat? Where's your fish-tail?'

'It's gone,' said Kimmy-Cat. 'Please don't talk of it to me, my friends. I am a good cat now, and all I want is to be kind and friendly.'

'We will be nice to you!' said the cats and dogs at once. 'If you will be nice to us, we will never say a word about the fish-tail, not one! Come and have some cream! And there's some nice boiled codfish that cook has got ready for us.'

'I'd like the cream – but not the fish!' said Kimmy-Cat with a shudder. And I'm not surprised, are you?

The Lambikin

There once was a Lambikin who frolicked about and had a lovely time. One day he set off to visit his Granny. He frisked along, thinking of all the lovely things she would give him,

when he met a Jackal.

'Hey, Lambikin, stop! I'll EAT you!' cried the Jackal. But the Lambikin jumped high into the air and cried: 'To my Granny's house I go, and I shall fatter grow, then you can eat me so.'

'Very well,' said the Jackal, and he let the Lambikin go on his way. Soon he met a Vulture, who shouted to the Lambikin: 'Hey, Lambikin, stop! I'll EAT you!'

But the Lambikin frisked round him and laughed: 'To my Granny's

house I go, and I shall fatter grow, then you can eat me so!'

'Very well,' said the Vulture, and he let the Lambikin go on his way.

Presently he met a Tiger, who called: 'Hey, Lambikin, stop! I'll EAT you!'

But the Lambikin jumped about on his four frisky legs and cried: 'To my Granny's house I go, and I shall fatter grow, then you can eat me so!'

'Very well,' said the Tiger, and he let the Lambikin go on his way. Soon the little creature came to his

Granny's house and he greeted her with joy.

'Granny,' he said, 'I've promised to get fat. So will you please put me in the corn-bin?'

His Granny popped him in there and he ate for seven days till he could eat no more.

'Granny,' he said, when he came out, 'I am so fat now that I am afraid I shall be eaten on my way home. Please make a drumikin for me, and put me inside.'

So his Granny made a drumikin for him out of a barrel with skin stretched over each end, and he set off home rolling along inside the drumikin.

Soon he met the Tiger, who called out: 'Drumikin, drumikin, have you seen Lambikin?'

'He's lost in the forest and so are

you. On, little drumikin! Tum-pa, tum-poo!' cried Lambikin.

'What a pity!' said the Tiger, and let the drumikin roll on its way.

Soon the Vulture flew down, and cried: 'Drumikin, drumikin, have you seen Lambikin?'

'He's lost in the forest and so are you. On, little drumikin! Tum-pa, tum-poo!' cried Lambikin.

'What a pity!' said the Vulture and let the drumikin roll on its way.

Soon the Jackal came up and cried: 'Drumikin, drumikin, have you seen

Lambikin?'

'He's lost in the forest and so are you. On, little drumikin! Tum-pa, tum-poo!' cried Lambikin.

But the Jackal knew Lambikin's voice and rushed after the drumikin. In a fright the Lambikin rolled the drumikin down the hill to his home

with the Jackal close after him. He bumped open the door of his house and got inside just in time. 'Tum-pa, tum-poo!' he cried.